DISCARD

TWO CAN PLAY

For Susan, thank you for all your advice,
pickles, and rice pudding.

American edition published in 2021 by Andersen Press USA,
an imprint of Andersen Press Ltd.
www.andersenpressusa.com

First published in Great Britain in 2021 by Andersen Press Ltd.,
20 Vauxhall Bridge Road, London SW1V 2SA.

Distributed in the United States and Canada by
Lerner Publishing Group, Inc.
241 First Avenue North
Minneapolis, MN 55401 USA

For reading levels and more information, look up this title at www.lernerbooks.com.

Library of Congress Cataloging-in-Publication Data Available

ISBN: 978-1-72842-413-2

1 - TOPPAN LEFUNG - 9/2020

TWO CAN PLAY

SCARY SCARECROWS

MARGARET STURTON

Andersen Press USA

"What are you doing?" asked Puss.

"I'm planning our garden," said Cat.
"We'll need to work together to
make it magnificent. It'll be fun."

"But I don't want to work, I want to play," said Puss. "That's much more fun."
"Working together is fun," said Cat.

"Come on. First we need to do some digging," said Cat.

"No!" said Puss.

So Cat dug the garden by herself.

Puss thought digging looked like hard work.

"Will you come and choose some seeds?" asked Cat.

"No!" said Puss.

So Cat got herself ready . . .

and cycled into Town.

THE BUN SHOP SUPER SOCKS SPROUT'S SEEDS TOPP T-SHIRTS

Cat chose the seeds she wanted.
Puss thought choosing seeds might actually
be a bit fun, but she would never say so.

"Will you help me plant the seeds?" asked Cat.

"No!" said Puss. "I told you, I just want to play!"

So Cat used her wheelbarrow
to collect what she needed . . .

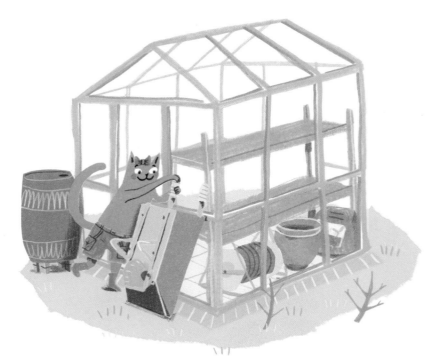

and prepared the soil.

Cat planted the seeds
outside and waited for
her plants to grow.

Secretly, Puss liked watching plants grow too, but she wasn't going to admit it.

"Will you help me scare the birds so they don't eat all the seedlings?" asked Cat.

"No!" said Puss. "That's not fun."

So Cat made model owls, chimes, and mirrors that flashed in the sunlight.

Puss was tempted to join in.

"Will you help me make dinner?" asked Cat.

"No thanks!" said Puss. "That sounds like work to me."

So Cat picked everything she needed to make a fine feast . . .

. . . and got to work in the kitchen. The cooking smells were wonderfully good.

"Please may I taste some?" purred Puss.

"Hmm . . ." said Cat.
"What do you think?"

"Perhaps . . . not," Puss said quietly. "Because
I didn't do any of the work, did I?

I'd better go and do
the washing-up."
Puss slowly walked
toward the kitchen.
"Hang on a minute,"
said Cat.

"Eating together
is far more fun
than eating alone.

So is playing while we do
the washing-up.

And storing the extra fruit and vegetables for the winter together is the best fun of all!"

"You know, I've always thought working together is the same as playing and having fun," said Puss. "Oh, really, is that so," said Cat. "I wasn't expecting that."